JACK and the BEANSTALK and the French Fries

by Mark Teague

Orchard Books · New York · An Imprint of Scholastic Inc.

To Kitty Scherbatsky

Library of Congress catalog card number: 2016037154
ISBN 978-0-545-91431-4
10 9 8 7 6 5 4 3 2 1   17 18 19 20 21

Printed in China 62
First edition, August 2017
Book design by Charles Kreloff and Steve Ponzo

Jack lived with his mother in a small house at the edge of a village. They were very poor. They were so poor that when their cow stopped giving milk, Jack's mother feared that they would starve. "Quickly, son," she said, "take the cow to market and sell her for as much as you can. Everything depends on it."

Jack lived with his mother in a small house at the edge of a village. They were very poor. They were so poor that when their cow stopped giving milk, Jack's mother feared that they would starve. "Quickly, son," she said, "take the cow to market and sell her for as much as you can. Everything depends on it."

Jack headed off with the cow in tow. After a while he stopped to rest, and when he did, a stranger appeared. "I will trade you these magic beans for that cow," said the old man. "Magic beans!" said Jack. "You must think I'm a dodo."

"Not at all," said the stranger. "And these beans are quite magical. Plant them and you will have all that you desire."

"Honest?" said Jack. What he desired at the moment was food.

"Honest," said the stranger. So they made the deal and Jack returned home with the beans.

"Foolish boy!" cried his mother. "You have ruined us."
She tossed the beans out a window and sent Jack to bed
without any supper.

When he awoke next morning, a strange light filled Jack's room.
Giant leaves poked through the window. He stuck his head out and
saw an enormous beanstalk growing in the backyard. "Ma!" he cried,
running downstairs. "Check out the beanstalk!"

"I already did. And look. I made us bean porridge for breakfast!"

Jack ate the porridge. It wasn't the best thing ever, but it beat
starving. "Well, I guess our problem is solved," he said, and headed
off to school.

After that, Jack and his mother ate beans all the time. They ate bean salad and bean soup, pickled beans and refried beans, baked beans, minced beans, mashed beans, breaded beans, bean sprouts, and bean dip. After a while, Jack grew tired of beans. He dreamed of burgers. He dreamed of french fries. "Couldn't we have something else?" he grumbled, staring at his bean chowder.

"Why would we want anything else?" said his mother. "Beans are nutritious and delicious and, best of all, they're free."

And thanks to the magic beanstalk, there were always more of them. The stalk produced enormous quantities of beans. They grew through the spring, the summer, and the fall. Even in winter they kept coming. Jack's mother shared beans with the neighbors and the neighbors' neighbors and the neighbors' neighbors' neighbors. Soon the entire village was eating them.

At first everyone seemed grateful, but the feeling didn't last. At dinnertime, Jack could hear the howls of children from blocks away. "Please!" they cried. "No more beans!"

School was even worse. Kids glared at him over their bean-filled lunches. His classmates said, "It's all your fault. You never should have planted that thing."

"I didn't!" said Jack. "Not really." But nobody believed him. Big kids threw bean sandwiches at him. Bullies chased him home from school. "This has to stop," he thought, but he didn't know what to do.

On his birthday, Jack was given a beanbag, a bean shooter, and a slice of bean cake topped with a dollop of ice bean. "That does it," he thought as he lay in bed. "The beanstalk has to go."

Next morning he grabbed a hatchet and stomped outside. He was about to give the stalk a good whack when the stranger appeared once again. "Wait," said the old man. "Aren't you curious what's up there?"

"I know what's up there," said Jack. "Beans."

"Don't be foolish," said the stranger. "Climb. Here, I'll give you a boost."

Just then an angry mob appeared at the end of
the street. Among them were the worst bullies
from school. They carried torches and pitchforks.
They chanted, "NO MORE BEANS!"

One of them spotted Jack. "Look, it's the bean kid!"

"Okay," said Jack, "I'll climb." He gave his hatchet
to the stranger and scrambled up the beanstalk.

Up and up he went, until the village looked small below him. Jack wasn't crazy about heights, but bullies were worse. He kept climbing. The beanstalk disappeared into a cloud. He realized he was hungry— for anything other than beans—but there was nothing to eat and no way to go but up.

Finally, the beanstalk arrived at the top of a cliff. From there, a path wandered off into the distance. Jack followed the path until he came to the front door of a huge castle. Hunger made him bold. "There must be food in here," he thought as he slipped inside.

Jack wandered gloomy hallways until he came to an immense kitchen. A giant woman stood at a wooden table. She was canning beans.

"Ugh," said Jack.

"What are you doing here?" she cried, dropping her can.

"I was hoping for something to eat."

"Silly boy! Don't you know where you are? My husband is a giant—Twice as big as me. And lately he's been very grumpy."

"I'll bet it's the beans," said Jack.

"Don't be ridiculous," she said. "Beans are nutritious and delicious and, best of all, they're free."

But Jack was right. Ever since the mighty stalk had appeared, the Giants had been eating nothing but beans. And Mr. Giant was sick of them.

Loud footsteps sounded in the hallway. "FEE FI FO—Say, what's for lunch?"

"Quick!" hissed Mrs. Giant. "You must hide."

Jack dove headfirst into a flour barrel. A moment later, Mr. Giant strode into the kitchen. "Boy, am I hungry!"

"Good," Mrs. Giant said. "I made you a nice bean salad."

"Bean salad!" he cried. "But all we ever have is beans. AND I HATE BEANS!"

"We love beans," she said. "And they're good for you. How do you think you got so big?"

"Dunno. But you eat 'em and you're puny."

"I'm busy," she said. "Now eat your salad and stop complaining."

The giant ate, but he didn't stop complaining. "Beans,"
he grumbled. "What I wouldn't give for a plate of french fries."
Without thinking, Jack said, "Hear, hear."
"What was that?" cried the giant, leaping to his feet.
"Nothing!" said his wife.
"I know what I heard! And it came from that flour barrel!" The giant
stomped over to the barrel and plucked Jack up by his feet. He turned
to his wife. "What is this?"
"It's just a boy," said Mrs. Giant. "He was looking for something to eat."
"Maybe he *is* something to eat. Look, he's already breaded."
"Don't be disgusting," she said.
"Yes," said Jack. "Don't be disgusting."

The giant set Jack on the table, but he was still angry. "You know what's disgusting? Beans." He dumped a bushel on his head. "You see? Disgusting." He overturned another bushel and another. He picked up great handfuls of beans and tossed them in the air. Soon, beans were flying everywhere. Jack joined in. They made a terrific mess, and as they did they chanted, "NO MORE BEANS!"

"Stop!" cried Mrs. Giant. "Both of you should be ashamed. If you don't like beans, plant something else."

"Plant?" said Jack.

"Something else?" said the giant.

"A vegetable garden, you ninnies. With potatoes, for instance."

"Why taters?" said her husband.

"To make french fries!" cried Jack. "Of course. We'll plant some right away."

"First you'll clean this kitchen," said Mrs. Giant.

As soon as they were done, they headed down the beanstalk.
The bullies were waiting at the bottom. "There he is!" they
cried when Jack appeared.
Jack wasn't worried. "Meet my friend," he said.
Once the uproar died down and the bullies went home,
Jack and the giant spent the rest of the day planting a garden.

"GROW!" shouted the giant.
"Patience," said Jack.
Soon the giant grew bored and headed back up the stalk. But Jack tended his garden every day. The vegetables grew and grew.

In fact, whatever magic had produced the beanstalk seemed to be working on the other plants as well. Before long the backyard was bursting with carrots, corn, potatoes, tomatoes, and asparagus. Everything was enormous.

There was so much food, they didn't know what to do, so Jack and his mother cooked up a feast. The smell spread across the village and all the way up the beanstalk. By dinnertime, everyone was there, even the giants. It was the most stupendous meal anyone could remember. They all agreed that the food was delicious and nutritious, and best of all . . .

. . . were the french fries.